HOVERING HELICOPTERS

For Louie Ronald Ellwood Cope – T.M.
For Wilf – A.P.

KINGFISHER

First published 2017 by Kingfisher,
an imprint of Macmillan Children's Books
20 New Wharf Road, London N1 9RR

ISBN 978-0-7534-4469-6

Text copyright © Tony Mitton 2016
Illustrations copyright © Ant Parker 2016
Designed by Anthony Hannant (LittleRedAnt) 2016

A CIP catalogue record for this book is available
from the British Library

Printed in China
9 8 7 6 5 4 3 2 1

HOVERING HELICOPTERS

Tony Mitton and
Ant Parker

KINGFISHER

Helicopters hovering,
hanging in the sky –

clattering and racketing,
they hover low and high.

A helicopter's rotor blades
create the lift and rise.

They press upon the air to send it
riding through the skies.

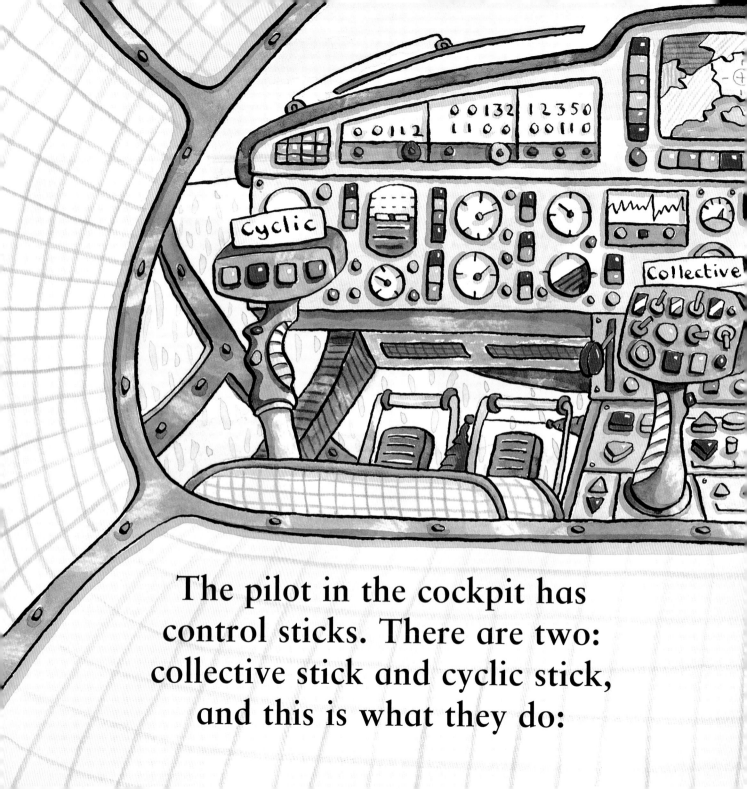

The pilot in the cockpit has
control sticks. There are two:
collective stick and cyclic stick,
and this is what they do:

collective sticks will take
a helicopter high or low;
cyclic sticks control the way
a copter needs to go.

For copters can go forwards,
backwards, sideways, up or down,

which means they're great for
tricky things in country or in town.

This copter is an ambulance.
When patients need quick care,
if roads are slow a copter
can deliver them by air.

This copter uses radar
to scan the stormy seas.

It winches crew to safety when they've
signalled, "Help us, please!"

This mountain rescue copter goes
to places high and snowy.

It rescues people stranded where the
weather's chill and blowy.

And here's a helicopter scooping
water from a lake.

You need a lot of water with
a forest fire to break.

Police use helicopters
to observe things on the ground.
Their cameras are good for trailing
cars and people round.

They sometimes use a searchlight
to show things on the go,
and radio their ground crew
who are busy down below.

This shuttle helicopter is
a taxi in the sky.

It's come to take us on a trip.
It's time to say good-bye.

Helicopter parts

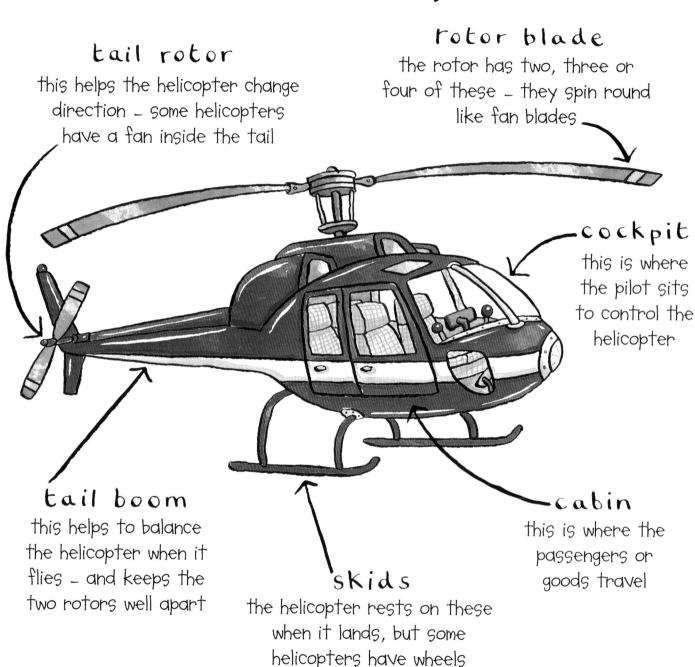

tail rotor
this helps the helicopter change direction — some helicopters have a fan inside the tail

rotor blade
the rotor has two, three or four of these — they spin round like fan blades

cockpit
this is where the pilot sits to control the helicopter

tail boom
this helps to balance the helicopter when it flies — and keeps the two rotors well apart

skids
the helicopter rests on these when it lands, but some helicopters have wheels

cabin
this is where the passengers or goods travel